High Sc
for Dummies

by Bradley Hayward

Baker's Plays
7611 Sunset Blvd.
Los Angeles, CA 90042
bakersplays.com

NOTICE

This book is offered for sale at the price quoted only on the understanding that, if any additional copies of the whole or any part are necessary for its production, such additional copies will be purchased. The attention of all purchasers is directed to the following: this work is fully protected under the copyright laws of the United States of America, the British Commonwealth, including Canada, and all other countries of the Copyright Union. Violations of the Copyright Law are punishable by fine or imprisonment, or both. The copying or duplication of this work or any part of this work, by hand or by any process, is an infringement of the copyright and will be vigorously prosecuted.

This play may not be produced by amateurs or professionals for public or private performance without first submitting application for performing rights. Licensing fees are due on all performances whether for charity or gain, or whether admission is charged or not. Since performance of this play without the payment of the licensing fee renders anybody participating liable to severe penalties imposed by the law, anybody acting in this play should be sure, before doing so, that the licensing fee has been paid. Professional rights, reading rights, radio broadcasting, television and all mechanical rights, etc. are strictly reserved. Application for performing rights should be made directly to BAKER'S PLAYS.

No one shall commit or authorize any act or omission by which the copyright of, or the right to copyright, this play may be impaired. No one shall make any changes in this play for the purpose of production.

Publication of this play does not imply availability for performance. Both amateurs and professionals considering a production are strongly advised in their own interest to apply to Baker's Plays for written permission before starting rehearsals, advertising, or booking a theatre.

Whenever the play is produced, the author's name must be carried in all publicity, advertising and programs. Also, the following notice must appear on all printed programs, "Produced by special arrangement with Baker's Plays."

Licensing fees for HIGH SCHOOL FOR DUMMIES are based on a per performance rate and payable one week in advance of the production.

Please consult the Baker's Plays website at www.bakersplays.com or our current print catalogue for up to date licensing fee information.

HIGH SCHOOL FOR DUMMIES
ISBN **978-0-87440-282-7**
#6317-B

AUTHOR'S NOTES

SETS

It is important that the play run swiftly and smoothly, which is why I recommend a simple set. However, it has also been produced fantastically with more elaborate settings. So if you have the resources and wherewithal to create a more complex set (so long as it remains fully functional), go for it!

STAGING

If using 8 actors to play all of the roles, none of them should ever leave the stage. Have the actors not participating in a given scene sit on stools to the side. For a larger cast, allow for standard exits and entrances.

COSTUMES

When doubling, dress the actors uniformly and then choose one or two distinct accessories to differentiate between characters. For a large cast, the options are endless.

LIGHTING

Feel free to use the suggested light cues, come up with your own, or eliminate them all together.

UPDATES

While I usually try to avoid dating my plays by making any references to contemporary pop culture, I did mention the hit Broadway musical "Mamma Mia." Should this musical close (but not until it does), please update the reference by substituting the latest Broadway juggernaut in its place.

CHARACTERS

Flexible cast of 8 to 32, (4-16 males; 4-16 females)

The ensemble is a core group of actors that may play many different characters. Alternately, you could choose to have a very large cast with each actor having a small role. If casting with 8 actors, the following is a suggested breakdown.

ACTOR 1 – **ONE, OWEN, JEFFREY, PAUL**
ACTOR 2 – **TWO, MARGE, JULIA, RHONDA**
ACTOR 3 – **THREE, DRIVER, TREVOR, RICH**
ACTOR 4 – **FOUR, MRS. GREEN, KRISTA, JACQUI**
ACTOR 5 – **FIVE, JASON, MARK, MR. HARRIS**
ACTOR 6 – **SIX, STEPH, VERONICA, ANNE**
ACTOR 7 – **SEVEN, NATHAN, DAVID, MR. JOHNSON**
ACTOR 8 – **EIGHT, LISA, BECKY, ELLE**

TIME

The present.

PLACE

A high school.

SCENE

A bare stage. Chairs and blocks may be arranged to suggest each setting, but keep it fast and furious.

(*LIGHTS up CS. Eight* **ACTORS** *stand in a line, dressed in caps and gowns. They each hold a yellow and black book from the "For Dummies" series in front of them.*)

ONE. Computers for Dummies.

TWO. French for Dummies.

THREE. Psychology for Dummies.

FOUR. Guitar for Dummies.

FIVE. Golf for Dummies.

SIX. Drawing for Dummies.

SEVEN. Poker for Dummies.

EIGHT. Dogs for Dummies.

ONE. Diabetes.

TWO. Religion.

THREE. Grilling.

FOUR. Knitting.

FIVE. Taxes.

SIX. Yoga.

SEVEN. Art.

EIGHT. Sex.

EVERYONE. For dummies!

ONE. Every time you turn around, there's yet another book –

EVERYONE. For dummies!

TWO. It makes you wonder if everyone in the world are –

EVERYONE. Dummies!

THREE. 24/7, you can order a book that shows you the proper way to train a dog.

FOUR. Or row a boat.

FIVE. Or limbo.

SIX. Millions of people shell out millions of dollars to find out millions of tips about millions of things that don't really matter.

SEVEN. But there's no how-to guide for the most difficult chore of them all.

EIGHT. The one thing that really does matter.

EVERYONE. High school!

ONE. Who do you turn to when you get stuffed in a locker?

TWO. What do you eat when the cafeteria serves mush?

THREE. Where do you hide when the principal calls you to the office?

FOUR. As graduating seniors, we've been there –

FIVE. Done that.

SIX. So for all the freshmen about to enter this crazy jungle, where nothing ever goes right, we have some advice to share.

SEVEN. A survival guide for those days when it seems like nobody cares.

EIGHT. The book teenagers have been waiting for. High school –

EVERYONE. For dummies!

ONE. Chapter one...

EVERYONE. The school bus!

> (*LIGHTS out. LIGHTS up CS, on a school bus. The* **DRIVER** *sits in front, with* **STEPH**, **JASON** *and* **LISA** *in the back. The road is very bumpy and they all bounce up and down like jack-hammers.*)

STEPH. (*Applying lipstick.*) It's the first day of school. I have to look my best! (*She holds out the lipstick.*) You want?

LISA. What if our parents find out? We're not allowed to wear make-up yet.

STEPH. Get with it, Lisa! What do they know? We're freshman now, so we can do what we want. Plus, we're so much more mature than last year. We're practically adults. (*She freaks out.*) Oh my god, is that glitter in your nail polish?! It's, like, so cute!

LISA. Yeah, I know!

STEPH. All the boys are gonna just die when they see it.

JASON. (*Peeking out from behind a book.*) Yeah, die laughing.

STEPH. Huh?

JASON. Will you two be good little girls and shut-up?

LISA. What's that supposed to mean?

JASON. It means I don't want to hear about your stupid glitter nail polish.

STEPH. You're just jealous because I'm not your girlfriend.

JASON. (*Sarcastic.*) Yeah right. I spent my whole summer vacation waiting to make out with a freshman.

STEPH. Bite me.

JASON. Grow up. (*He returns to his book.*)

STEPH. What a jerk.

LISA. Maybe he's right.

STEPH. About what?

LISA. Maybe we do need to grow up. Give me some of that lipstick.

STEPH. Really?

LISA. I better, if I want any of the boys to look at me. Besides, I'll wash it off before I go home. Mom will never find out.

STEPH. Yay! You'll look, like, so pretty!

(**LISA** *starts to put on lipstick when the bus hits a pothole. They all bounce out of their seats. In the process,* **LISA** *smears a big streak of lipstick across her face.*)

LISA. Oh no! Look what happened!

STEPH. What?

LISA. The lipstick! Did it leave a mark?

STEPH. Oh my god. It's all over your face.

LISA. How bad is it?

STEPH. Bad. You look like an Easter egg.

LISA. Well, quick! Help me get it off!

(*As they search for tissues,* **JASON** *laughs uproariously.*)

STEPH. What are you laughing at?

JASON. You twits are so immature.

STEPH. And you're a moron.

LISA. Stop arguing and wash it off!

(**STEPH** *spits into a tissue and furiously rubs* **LISA***'s face.*)

JASON. Aw, that's so cute. Mommy's washing your face.

LISA. Is it coming off?

STEPH. Let me see. (*She checks.*) No. Still there.

LISA. Let me try! (*She continues scrubbing.*)

STEPH. (*Looking at the lipstick.*) Oh no.

LISA. What?

STEPH. It's waterproof.

LISA. What?! You mean I have to go all day like this? Mom's going to find out for sure.

JASON. Serves you right for being so stupid.

STEPH. That's it! I've had enough of you!

JASON. (*Stands up.*) Oh yeah?

STEPH. (*Stands up.*) Yeah! (*They hit another bump and* **STEPH** *falls into* **JASON***'s lap. They start fighting.*)

JASON. Get off me!

STEPH. Not until you apologize!

DRIVER. Hey, what's going on back there? (**ONE** *emerges from the darkness. He steps into the scene and shouts.*)

ONE. Freeze! (**EVERYONE** *in the bus freezes. He speaks to the audience.*) Page 8. When confronted with a nasty bus ride, the solution is simple. Convince the driver to take the highway. Not only is the road less bumpy, but the trip is ten minutes shorter. And it's all smooth sailing from there. (*As he sits behind the* **DRIVER***, they all unfreeze and resume bouncing. He leans over the* **DRIVER***'s shoulder.*) Hey, driver.

DRIVER. Stay back. If you cross the yellow line, I have to pull over.

ONE. I'll stay behind the yellow line if you take the highway.

DRIVER. Sorry, kiddo. I've got my route to stick to.

ONE. Come on. These vibrations must be killing your butt.

DRIVER. Yes, but I still have two students to pick up. Nathan Chell and Owen Jones.

ONE. Why bother? Nobody likes them, anyway.

DRIVER. It's not my job to judge. I just drive them to school.

ONE. You'd be singing a different tune if you knew what I know.

DRIVER. What do you know?

ONE. Remember last Halloween? (*He nods.*) Remember the eggs on your new car? The ones that ruined the paint job? (*He nods.*) That was Nathan.

DRIVER. So what? All kids pull stuff like that.

ONE. And remember the boy you found in your house? (*He nods.*) The one in your daughter's bedroom? (*He nods, getting angry.*) The one who got away before you saw his face? (*He nods, raving mad.*) That was Owen.

DRIVER. It was? (**ONE** *nods.*) Where's the on-ramp?

ONE. Straight ahead. (*The* **DRIVER** *steers onto the highway.*) My work here is done. (*He sits back in his seat. They all stop bouncing.*)

STEPH. Whew! It looks like I got it all off.

LISA. Thanks. It would have sucked to look like a clown all day. Now that it's not so bumpy, maybe you can help me put it on straight.

STEPH. Sure. This is going to be, like, the best first day ever!

JASON. (*Peeking out from behind his book.*) That's what they all say.

(*As* **STEPH** *helps* **LISA** *with the lipstick, LIGHTS out. LIGHTS up DR, on* **TWO**.)

TWO. Now if you think getting to school is difficult, things only get worse when you finally arrive. Set foot in a classroom and it's no longer a matter of you versus them. It's you versus Mister or Missus Them. Enter the teachers. Chapter two...

EVERYONE. Attendance!

(*LIGHTS out. LIGHTS up CS, on a classroom.* **NATHAN** *and* **OWEN** *sit in the back row.* **BECKY** *sits in the front.* **MRS. GREEN** *drones on from her desk.*)

MRS. GREEN. Nathan Chell.

NATHAN. Here.

MRS. GREEN. Owen Jones.

OWEN. Here.

MRS. GREEN. Becky Heard.

(**NATHAN** *chuckles as he puts a straw to his lips. He shoots a spit ball at the back of* **BECKY***'s head.*)

BECKY. Hey!

(**NATHAN** *and* **OWEN** *burst into laughter.* **MRS. GREEN** *it not pleased.*)

MRS. GREEN. When I call your name, the answer is "here." Not "present." Not "yes." And certainly not "hey."

BECKY. But Nathan blew a spit ball at me.

MRS. GREEN. I do not care if he blew pop rocks at you. You will answer like a lady. Let us try this again. Becky Heard.

BECKY. (*Angrily.*) Here.

OWEN. Heard the turd.

BECKY. Shut-up!

MRS. GREEN. Miss Heard, I will not tolerate such profanity in my classroom.

BECKY. But he called me Heard the turd.

MRS. GREEN. That is no excuse. Vulgarity is a sure fire route to the principal's office. You do not want that, now do you?

BECKY. No.

MRS. GREEN. Very well. (*She checks her book.*) Wait a moment. Miss Heard, it looks like you are not obeying my seating assignments.

BECKY. I know. That's because Owen hocked a loogey on my chair.

MRS. GREEN. He hocked a what-y?

BECKY. A loogey.

MRS. GREEN. (*Shaking her head.*) I do not know what has gotten into you, young lady, but I will not stand for all of this confounded slang. I may be getting up in years, but I know a curse word when I hear one.

BECKY. Loogey's not a curse.

MRS. GREEN. I do not know what it is. And quite frankly, I do not care. Whatever it is, it does not give you the right to interfere with my diagram. Now take your appointed seat.

BECKY. But, Mrs. Green, it's all wet.

MRS. GREEN. So?

BECKY. And sticky.

MRS. GREEN. I have had it about up to here with your ignorance. Young girls who cannot follow authority are the ones that end up with a family of four by the time they are eighteen. I must put a stop to this, so here is a hall pass. Take this directly to the principal for your punishment.

BECKY. Please, no! I'll sit in the right seat, okay? (*Pause.*)

MRS. GREEN. Very well. But this is your last chance. I will have you know that you are treading around on very thin ice. (**BECKY** *reluctantly stands and approaches the boys.* **NATHAN** *chuckles.*)

NATHAN. Heard the turd.

(**BECKY** *turns to tell on him, but thinks better of it. She slowly sits down, absolutely disgusted. She wiggles around on the spit.*)

BECKY. (*Almost in tears.*) Mrs. Green, this is really gross.

MRS. GREEN. What did you say, Miss Heard?!

BECKY. Nothing. Nothing at all.

(**NATHAN** *and* **OWEN** *roar with laughter.* **TWO** *steps into the scene.*)

TWO. Freeze! (**EVERYONE** *freezes.*) Page 21. Imitation is the sincerest form of flattery. When faced with a brutal teacher, it is best to take on their most potent attributes. You will also obtain precious bonus points for complimenting them at length on the exact things that annoy you most. (*She sits in* **BECKY***'s original seat.* **EVERYONE** *unfreezes.*)

MRS. GREEN. Samantha Ryan.

TWO. Here. And might I add that you look wonderful in that tweed suit. It brings out the beautiful color of that mole on your nose.

MRS. GREEN. (*Deeply touched.*) Why, thank you, Samantha.

TWO. You are most welcome. Might I also add that I agree with you, Mrs. Green. Becky Heard is on a downward spiral into oblivion. If she does not clean up her act, she is most definitely headed to Lamaze class by senior year.

MRS. GREEN. I am glad to hear you say that.

TWO. And I have just the solution to prevent her from breast feeding at the prom.

MRS. GREEN. I would love to hear it.

TWO. Separate her from those two misfits in the back.

MRS. GREEN. And disrupt my seating assignments?

TWO. I know it sounds drastic. But drastic times call for drastic measures. Owen is a filthy pig and Nathan is full of spit. They are to blame for Becky's misfortune.

MRS. GREEN. Do you really think so?

TWO. I do. And might I add that your watch makes those liver spots look fabulous.

MRS. GREEN. (*Grinning from ear to ear.*) Very well. Samantha and Becky, please change seats. (**BECKY** *and* **TWO** *change seats.* **BECKY** *whispers as they pass.*)

BECKY. Thank you.

TWO. My pleasure.

(*They sit.* **NATHAN** *blows another spit ball at* **BECKY** *and laughs.*)

OWEN. Heard the turd.

MRS. **GREEN**. I saw that, Mr. Chell! And I heard that, Mr. Jones! It is directly to the principal's office for the both of you! How dare you influence a sweet and delicate flower such as Miss Heard.

(**NATHAN** *and* **OWEN** *are shocked. They glare at* **BECKY** *as they exit, and she chuckles. LIGHTS out. LIGHTS up DR, on* **THREE.**)

THREE. Now that you've been signed in to a day of torture, it's time to check your schedule. Horror strikes when you find out the first class of the day is gym. In junior high, this would have been merely a blip in the radar. But between the eighth and ninth grades, puberty takes hold. Freshmen become stinky, sweaty creatures that require hourly applications of deodorant. And with gym in the morning, there's no evading the showers. Chapter three...

EVERYONE. Gym class!

(*LIGHTS out. LIGHTS up CS, on a gymnasium.* **MARK**, **DAVID** *and* **JEFFREY** *stand in a triangle. They each have a ball and toss them back and forth on each line of dialogue.*)

MARK. You first.

DAVID. No, you first.

JEFFREY. No, you first.

MARK. Someone has to go first.

DAVID. Well, I'm not going first.

JEFFREY. And neither am I.

MARK. Come on, we're all freshmen here.

DAVID. I guess.

JEFFREY. Then what are we worried about?

MARK. I have no idea.

DAVID. So are we doing it, or what?

JEFFREY. Okay. Let's shower together.

> (*They toss the balls, but are so grossed out that all three bounce to the floor.* **THREE** *steps into the scene.*)

THREE. Freeze! (**EVERYONE** *freezes.*) Page 45. Make peace with your body hair. It's not going anywhere, and will only multiply as time goes on. For girls, this leads to strange shaving rituals at pajama parties. For boys, however, the problem is far more complex. There's nobody to come at them with razors, so they keep it to themselves. Thus, the only way to come to terms with such follicles is to think of it from a girl's perspective. (*He picks up a ball.* **EVERYONE** *unfreezes.*) Hey guys! Can I play?

MARK. Sure.

THREE. So what's going on?

DAVID. (*Paranoid.*) Nothing! We're just friends!

JEFFREY. Yeah, we're not doing anything weird.

THREE. Touchy, touchy. I was just wondering. You guys seem a little on edge.

MARK. Well, we're not!

THREE. I thought it was because those girls were watching you.

DAVID. What girls?

THREE. (*Points.*) Over there. I heard them whispering and they really like your muscles.

JEFFREY. (*Flexing.*) Really?

THREE. They said you guys were, "like, such hotties." I thought you were getting ready to ask them out.

MARK. We were.

DAVID. That's right!

JEFFREY. Those girls are hot! Come on, guys. Let's go. (*They start to strut away, as sexy as possible.*)

THREE. You're not going over there like that, are you? (*They stop dead in their tracks.*)

MARK. Like what?

THREE. You guys reek. Big time.

DAVID. We don't reek. (*To the* **GUYS**.) I don't smell, do I?

(*He lifts his arms up. The other two each sniff an armpit.*)

MARK. Ew, gross!

JEFFREY. That's foul, man!

DAVID. Let me smell you guys.

(**MARK** *and* **JEFFREY** *lift their arms.* **DAVID** *sniffs both of their armpits.*)

Oh god, that's disgusting! We could burn three holes in the ozone layer.

THREE. Then what are you waiting for? Wash up. Those girls aren't going to wait forever.

MARK. He's right. Let's hit the showers.

DAVID. Awesome. But we're still macho, right?

JEFFREY. Hotties like us? Oh, yeah!

(*They all slick their hair and flex for the girls. LIGHTS out. LIGHTS up DR, on* **FOUR**.)

FOUR. Between physical exertion and mental anguish, gym class burns a lot of calories. This is where nutrition plays a key role in one's stamina. It takes a lot of perseverance to fit in, but it takes even more tenacity to stomach a school lunch. Chapter four...

EVERYONE. The cafeteria!

(*LIGHTS out. LIGHTS up CS, on a cafeteria lunch line.* **MARGE**, *a grouch in a hair net, plops a glob of green gunk on* **VERONICA***'s tray.*)

MARGE. That enough, girly?

VERONICA. That depends. What is it?

MARGE. Mac and cheese.

VERONICA. But it's green.

MARGE. So?

VERONICA. So shouldn't it be closer to orange?

MARGE. This ain't no fancy two-star restaurant, missy. We don't follow no color chart.

VERONICA. Then, yes. That's plenty.

MARGE. You want any meat?

VERONICA. What kind?

MARGE. Brown.

VERONICA. I mean, is it chicken or beef?

MARGE. How should I know? Where I come from, meat is meat.

VERONICA. You mean it's just... brown?

MARGE. With flecks of green in it.

VERONICA. Then I think I'll pass.

MARGE. Your loss. But if you change your mind, make sure to come back by twelve thirty.

VERONICA. Why?

MARGE. It expires at one. (**TREVOR** *arrives at the front of the line.*)

TREVOR. Hi, Marge. I'll have three scoops of green and one hunk of brown.

MARGE. Coming right up.

TREVOR. (*To* **VERONICA.**) You're new, aren't you?

VERONICA. Yeah. I'm a freshman.

TREVOR. I figured. The cute ones always are.

VERONICA. (*Blushes.*) Thank you.

MARGE. (*Handing* **TREVOR** *his tray.*) There ya go, Trev. Eat up.

TREVOR. My name's Trevor, by the way.

VERONICA. I'm Veronica.

TREVOR. Would you like to sit with me and my friends, Veronica?

VERONICA. You mean it?

TREVOR. Sure do. (*He drops his fork.*) Oops. Could you get that for me? My hands are full.

VERONICA. (*Smitten.*) Sure!

> (*As she bends over to pick it up,* **TREVOR** *opens the flap on her book bag. He dumps the bowl of green gunk inside. He high fives* **MARGE**. **VERONICA** *stands up and hands him the fork, oblivious to his prank.*)

TREVOR. Thanks, Veronica. Anyone ever call you Ronnie?

VERONICA. No. (*Quickly.*) But you can if you want!

TREVOR. Okay. What about Vomit?

VERONICA. Huh?

TREVOR. Anyone ever call you Vomiting Veronica?

VERONICA. Why would they?

TREVOR. Check your bag, sucker! (*She opens her bag and finds the green gunk. She bursts into tears.*)

VERONICA. Why did you do that? This was my favorite bag.

MARGE. I guess he liked it, too, and was *green* with envy!

> (*She and* **TREVOR** *high five again.* **FOUR** *walks into the scene.*)

FOUR. Freeze! (**EVERYONE** *freezes.*) Page 63. Never, under any circumstances, eat the cafeteria food. It's never edible and only good for last minute biology projects. More importantly, the cafeteria is the most heinous room in the entire school. Devious behavior is so much more devious around salmonella. And lunch ladies can be the most underhanded of them all. However, if you know how to play your cards right, there's a very simple way around them.

> (*She grabs a tray and steps to the front of the line.* **EVERYONE** *unfreezes.*)

MARGE. Hey, no cutting!

FOUR. Marge, how come you're not a teacher?

MARGE. Did you hear me? I said no cutting.

FOUR. Wouldn't you rather be Mrs. Marge?

TREVOR. Are you deaf? Move to the back of the line!

FOUR. Then us kids might stop calling you names.

VERONICA. What are you doing?

FOUR. Just pay attention.

MARGE. (*Offended.*) They call me names? Like what?

FOUR. Large Marge, the lunch lady.

MARGE. But nobody calls me names. I'm the bully!

FOUR. And you always have been, right?

MARGE. You're darned tootin'. Nobody pushes me around.

FOUR. But that didn't get you very far, did it? You've been at this same counter for twenty years.

MARGE. Yeah. But so have these nuggets.

FOUR. The truth is, you really wanted to be a teacher. Isn't that right... Large Marge?

MARGE. (*Breaking down.*) Yes! You're right! I used to be like Veronica here. All the kids picked on me. So I fought back. But that got me expelled from school. Twenty years later and I'm stuck here, slinging various colors of crap onto all your crusty little trays.

TREVOR. Come on, Marge. Don't let her get you down. Let's slingshot some tapioca at the chess club!

MARGE. (*To* **TREVOR.**) And it's all because of kids like you!

TREVOR. What did I do?

MARGE. Robbed me of my future, that's what! Now take a bite, Trevor. Then you'll be the one vomiting. And if you think I'm dangerous, just wait till you see the nurse!

(**TREVOR** *storms off, whimpering.* **MARGE** *hands* **FOUR** *some cash as she takes the tray.*)

Don't eat this sludge, dearie, or you'll see it again by fourth period. Take this cash and buy yourself a real lunch.

FOUR. (*Handing* VERONICA *the money.*) Here you go. There's a Dairy Queen next door. Eat up!

(*LIGHTS out. LIGHTS up DR, on* FIVE.)

FIVE. Another thing changes between junior and senior high. The curriculum. Suddenly, you're faced with enormous academic expectations. To prepare you for college, teachers often leave students to their own devices when it comes to problem solving. Gone are the days when you can ask the same questions over and over. Unless, of course, those questions are rhetorical. High school teachers eat that up. Chapter five...

EVERYONE. Class!

(*LIGHTS out. LIGHTS up CS, on a classroom.* ELLE *and* KRISTA *sit cross-legged on the floor.* MR. JOHNSON *circles them, gesturing dramatically with his arms.*)

MR. JOHNSON. Let me pose a question. A question that has rumbled the world for generations. A question that has started wars... burned cities... ravaged nations. (*He holds up two drama masks, comedy and tragedy.*) What is drama?

(ELLE *raises her hand excitedly, but* MR. JOHNSON *pushes it down slowly.*)

No, no. Take your time. This question deserves careful and meticulous consideration.

(ELLE *has no idea what he means. She looks at* KRISTA, *but she just chomps on gum and blows a bubble. She waits and waits. Then sticks in her own piece of gum. Finally, she checks her watch and raises her hand again.*)

Now that you've given it deep thought, you may proceed.

ELLE. (*Proudly.*) Drama is a prose or verse composition that is intended for representation by actors impersonating the characters and performing the dialogue and action.

(*She's pleased with herself.* **MR. JOHNSON**, *however, is horrified. He crouches down, puts his glasses on the end of his nose and gives her a nasty glare.*)

MR. JOHNSON. Are you sure about that?

ELLE. Sure, I'm sure. That's what it says online. I read up on my classes all summer long!

MR. JOHNSON. (*Slowly turning to* **KRISTA**.) Do you agree with Elle's definition of drama?

(**KRISTA** *shrugs. Then she blows another bubble and lets it explode all over her face.*)

Very well.

(*He begins to chuckle. Quietly at first, and then loud and demonic like the devil.*)

ELLE. Is something wrong, Mr. Johnson?

MR. JOHNSON. I'll tell you what's wrong. You are! It's intellect like yours that has ailed this world for generations. Drama is greater than any definition you'll find on Google.

ELLE. It is?

MR. JOHNSON. Of course, silly girl. Why, if Robert E. Lee had brushed up on his Shakespeare, there would never have been a Civil War. And World War II could have been stopped, if only Hitler read "Hamlet."

ELLE. Are you kidding me?

MR. JOHNSON. Ignorance is bliss. (*He puts on the comic mask.*) But your innocence is tragic.

(*He switches to the drama mask.* **FIVE** *steps into the scene.*)

FIVE. Freeze! (**EVERYONE** *freezes.*) Page 80. Textbooks are a waste of time. You can figure out everything you need to know from class discussions. This is especially true for teachers who believe such books are propaganda. Simply wait for one of your classmates to voice an opinion, then disagree with it. The teacher will anyway, so it's best to get a head start. This trick always throws them for a loop.

(*He sits on the floor.* **EVERYONE** *unfreezes.*)

MR. JOHNSON. Would anyone like to take a crack at the meaning of upstaging?

ELLE. I will! Upstaging is improperly taking attention from an actor who should be the focus of interest.

(**FIVE** *raises his hand.*)

MR. JOHNSON. Yes, Anthony?

FIVE. That's the stupidest thing I've ever heard.

MR. JOHNSON. (*Pleased.*) Really? I didn't expect this. Perhaps my lectures aren't dissolving into thin air, after all. What do you think upstaging means?

FIVE. The exact opposite of what she said. Like, duh!

MR. JOHNSON. What keen insight you have. Everyone, take note of this young man's superior intellect.

ELLE. But he didn't say anything.

MR. JOHNSON. Far more than you've ever said. You could learn a thing or two from his wisdom. (*To* **FIVE**.) You're headed for greatness, young man. And do you know where great minds of this country belong?

FIVE. No. Where?

MR. JOHNSON. The Broadway stage! Why, this country would be a greater democracy, if only we'd elect a president from the cast of "Mamma Mia."

FIVE. Actually, Mr. Johnson, I can't take all the credit. You see, I was up studying all night with Elle. She's the one who said... well, whatever it was I said.

MR. JOHNSON. You can't fool me, you brilliant genius of man.

FIVE. Honest. But I convinced her that you'd prefer the textbook definition. Obviously, I was wrong.

MR. JOHNSON. Is that so, Elle? Are you the genius?

(**ELLE** *doesn't know what to say.* **FIVE** *gives her a firm jab in the side.*)

ELLE. Yes! I'm the one who said... well, whatever it was he said.

MR. JOHNSON. (*Cupping his ear.*) What's that I hear? Ah, yes! It's your applause. The footlights are waiting for you, Elle. Time to take a bow.

(**ELLE** *bows for an imaginary audience.* Then **KRISTA** *raises her hand.*)

Krista! You've elected to speak. This really is a big day. Do you have something you'd like to add to Elle's profound observations?

KRISTA. (*Takes the gum out of her mouth and stretches it.*) I've chewed the hell out of my gum. You got any Juicy Fruit?

(*LIGHTS out. LIGHTS up DR, on* **SIX.**)

SIX. After a mental workout, it's best to let your mind cool down a little. But when teenagers stop concentrating, even for a moment, their imaginations drift toward one subject, and one subject only. Sex. Suddenly those diagrams from Sex-Ed take on a whole new significance. And it's impossible to cool down when your cheeks are beet red. Chapter six...

EVERYONE. Sex!

(*LIGHTS out. LIGHTS up CS, on a bench.* **PAUL** *and* **JULIA** *nervously hold hands.*)

PAUL. We've been going steady for a real long time now. Forever, actually.

JULIA. I know. Three weeks.

PAUL. I like you. And you like me. So I was thinking...

JULIA. Yeah?

PAUL. Maybe it's time we go to second base. (**JULIA** *giggles.*) What? Did I say something funny?

JULIA. No. I just don't know much about football.

PAUL. Apparently you don't know anything about football. Cause that's baseball.

JULIA. Really? I'm so stupid.

PAUL. You're not stupid. I'll try again. But this time so you'll understand what I mean.

JULIA. Okay.

PAUL. Let's say our relationship is like make-up. So far, all we've done is lip gloss. I was thinking... only if you want... that we could try a little mascara.

JULIA. (*Gasps.*) Mom would kill me!

PAUL. Calm down!

JULIA. She's, like, super anti make-up. Last year, she said I needed to take on some responsibility, so she bought me a goldfish. But then I was grounded for giving it a filthy name.

PAUL. What did you call it?

JULIA. Max Factor.

PAUL. All I'm trying to say is... you're very pretty.

JULIA. Tell that to my mom.

PAUL. So would you...

JULIA. Would I what?

PAUL. Would you like to kiss me?

JULIA. (*Frustrated.*) Well, I don't know. Now you've got me thinking about mascara.

PAUL. Maybe I shouldn't have brought this up.

JULIA. Maybe not.

(**PAUL** *lets go of her hands and buries his face in his own, embarrassed.* **JULIA** *crosses her arms.* **SIX** *walks into the scene.*)

SIX. Freeze! (**EVERYONE** *freezes.*) Page 94. When it comes to sex, take it slow. Real slow. Sex is a far bigger step than choosing the right shade of blush. Just like in baseball, if you try to steal home, there's no going back. Move too soon and you'll get knocked out of the inning. But stay right where you are and maturity will soon be at bat.

(*She squishes between* **JULIA** *and* **PAUL**. **EVERYONE** *unfreezes.*)

What's with you guys?

PAUL & JULIA. (*Angrily.*) Nothing.

SIX. Come on. You can tell me.

PAUL. She doesn't like me, that's what.

JULIA. I never said that! I just got scared.

SIX. (*To* **PAUL**.) You want to kiss her, right?

PAUL. Yeah. What's wrong with that?

SIX. Nothing. (*To* **JULIA**.) But you've never kissed a guy before, have you?

JULIA. Just my grandpa. After my junior high graduation, he planted a sloppy one on my cheek. And he smelled like Fixodent. At first, I thought it was from his dentures. But it turns out he uses it to glue on his toupee.

PAUL. (*Laughing.*) I wonder if all his body parts are removable!

SIX. If you're still making jokes about body parts, you're not ready for sex.

PAUL. Ew, gross! Who said anything about sex?

SIX. Nobody. But when sex does come up, make sure you're ready for it.

PAUL. I'll totally gag if you keep talking about this.

SIX. Fine. For now, just go to the movies, hold hands, and giggle a lot. There's plenty of time for the rest later.

PAUL. Okay.

JULIA. So what do you say? A movie?

PAUL. Yeah. That sounds like fun.

(**SIX** *grabs their hands and clasps them together. They smile.*)

JULIA. But no mascara.

PAUL. No mascara.

SIX. That's it for me.

(*He raises their connected hands and ducks below them.*)

Three's a crowd.

(*She exits as* **PAUL** *and* **JULIA** *giggle. LIGHTS out. LIGHTS up DR, on* **SEVEN**.)

SEVEN. Let's be honest, freshmen can be obnoxious from time to time. So it's inevitable that at some time or other you'll have to make that long walk to the principal's office. Principals are never in a good mood, and it's been proven that their breath always smells like tuna. However, if you've been summoned to their office, you probably deserve it. Chapter seven...

EVERYONE. The principal!

(*LIGHTS out. LIGHTS up CS, on a principal's office.* **MR. HARRIS** *looms over* **RHONDA** *and* **JACQUI**, *with a stack of crumpled papers.*)

MR. HARRIS. I hope you understand the severity of your actions. In my school, passing notes in class is a criminal offense. Unless you wish to spend hard time in detention, I suggest you get your stories straight. (*Nose to nose with* **RHONDA**.) Now start talking. (**RHONDA** *stifles a laugh.*) Is something funny?

RHONDA. No.

(*Then* **JACQUI** *begins to giggle.* **MR. HARRIS** *glares at her and she immediately stops.*)

MR. HARRIS. (*Nose to nose with* **JACQUI**.) Do you have something you'd like to share with me?

JACQUI. Yeah. A Tic-Tac.

(*They both double over with laughter and cannot stop.* **MR. HARRIS** *produces a yard stick and slams it on his desk. They shut-up instantly.*)

MR. HARRIS. Students like you get my intestines in a twist. So listen up, kiddos. This isn't junior high anymore. Just like Bran Flakes, those cutesy smiles have no effect on me. Your last principal may have been a pushover, but nobody messes with Mr. Harris. This is my kingdom. My rules. If this be the Emerald City, then I be the great and powerful Oz! And neither of you are going home until I say so. You got that?

RHONDA. Got it, Wiz.

JACQUI. (*As the Wicked Witch.*) And you're little dog, too.

MR. HARRIS. If you so much as say another word out of turn, I will hold you ladies in contempt. Understand? (*They nod, biting their lips.*) Good. Now explain to me the meaning of these notes.

RHONDA. They don't mean anything. Honest.

MR. HARRIS. I highly doubt that. Let's take a look, shall we? (*He reads the notes one by one.*) "Hot dog. Mailbox. Tulip. Goat."

JACQUI. So?

MR. HARRIS. So it's some sort of code. A secret language to fool the entire faculty, I'm sure. Well, I hate to put a wrench in your plans, but I've got the English teacher working on it.

RHONDA. You have?

MR. HARRIS. Oh, yes. And it's only a matter of time before she figures it out. She's got a way with words. During staff meetings, she kills at Scattergories.

JACQUI. So what do you want from us?

MR. HARRIS. If you fess up now, I may be inclined to lessen your punishment.

RHONDA. Well... if you really wanna know.

MR. HARRIS. I really wanna know.

JACQUI. Okay. You know how teachers lean against the blackboard and end up with chalk all over their rear ends? Well, the smudges sort of look like clouds.

RHONDA. So we started looking for shapes. Those were the ones we found so far.

MR. HARRIS. A hot dog, a mailbox, a tulip, *and* a goat?

JACQUI. Yeah. Miss Wagner has a really big butt.

MR. HARRIS. And you think this is appropriate behavior?

RHONDA. Well, it was art class.

(*They break up all over again.* **MR. HARRIS** *remains stone faced.*)

JACQUI. Come on. You gotta admit that's funny!

MR. HARRIS. No. (*He raises the yard stick again.*) Not one bit. (**SEVEN** *steps into the scene.*)

SEVEN. Freeze! (**EVERYONE** *freezes.*) Page 106. If you get the principal to laugh, you're home free. Unfortunately, this is not an easy task. They get their jollies by telling lame jokes at the water-cooler. As it turns out, principals want to be popular, too. They desperately seek the approval of their staff, and will go to great lengths to achieve it. So if you've got a groaner that will put the librarian in stitches, fire away.

(*He gets ready to grab the yard stick as it comes down.* **EVERYONE** *unfreezes.*)

MR. HARRIS. I've had it up to here with you two!

SEVEN. (*Grabbing the yard stick.*) Careful, now. You don't want to hurt anyone. Although, you know what they say... to get results, you sometimes have to go to great "lengths." Get it? (*He holds up the ruler.*) Lengths?

(**MR. HARRIS** *chuckles. Then catches himself and returns his face to a scowl.*)

RHONDA. Did you just smile?

MR. HARRIS. No.

JACQUI. Yeah, you did. I saw it.

SEVEN. I've got another one for you. (*To the* **GIRLS**.) Name two pronouns.

RHONDA. Who? Me?

(**MR. HARRIS** *laughs again, a little harder. He holds his hand over his mouth to hide it.*)

JACQUI. There it is again!

RHONDA. By golly, he has teeth.

MR. HARRIS. (*About to burst.*) I'm not laughing.

SEVEN. Help me out, girls!

RHONDA & JACQUI. How?

SEVEN. No matter what I ask, I want you both to answer at once. What's four plus four?

RHONDA & JACQUI. (*Blankly.*) At once.

(**MR. HARRIS** *gives in and rolls on the floor, in tears.*)

JACQUI. That's all it takes?

MR. HARRIS. (*Getting the hiccups.*) Stop! Before Metamucil comes out my nose!

RHONDA. Let me try. (*Like a comedian.*) Hey, Jacqui. What do you get when you cross a teacher with a vampire?

JACQUI. I don't know. What do you get when you cross a teacher with a vampire?

RHONDA. Lots of blood tests!

(**MR. HARRIS** *goes into more spasms.*)

MR. HARRIS. Go on! I can't have you seeing me like this!

RHONDA. You mean we're not in trouble?

MR. HARRIS. No. So long as you don't breathe a word of this to your friends.

JACQUI. Not a peep.

RHONDA. (*To* **SEVEN.**) You rock my world.

SEVEN. Don't mention it.

(**RHONDA** *and* **JACQUI** *exit as* **MR. HARRIS** *slaps his thigh.*)

MR. HARRIS. Blood tests! Ha, ha, ha! Just wait till the faculty hears this.

(*LIGHTS out. LIGHTS up DR, on* **EIGHT.**)

EIGHT. Whew! The day is nearly over. The bright light at the end of the tunnel is finally close enough to make you squint. Unfortunately, it's not the end of your worries. You've heard all that stuff about peer pressure. But the word "peer" is only uttered by those who never had any friends in high school. People with active social lives don't go around saying, "You wanna come to my sleep-over? All our *peers* will be there." They're your friends. And no matter what age you are, you can never have too many. Chapter eight...

EVERYONE. Friendship!

(*LIGHTS out. LIGHTS up CS, on a detention hall.* **ANNE** *writes on a sheet of paper.*)

ANNE. "I will not kick the cheerleaders. I will not kick the cheerleaders. I will not kick the cheerleaders."

(**RICH** *barges in. He glares at* **ANNE** *and taps his foot for a long time. She can't take it anymore.*)

What do you want?!

RICH. You're in my seat.

ANNE. This isn't your seat.

RICH. Yeah it is.

ANNE. Buzz off! (*She writes some more.*) "I will not kick the cheerleaders."

RICH. If I say it's my seat, it's my seat!

ANNE. Nobody has their own seat in detention. "I will not kick the cheerleaders."

RICH. I do!

ANNE. Who says?

RICH. I says. When it comes to detention, I make the rules.

ANNE. Listen up! I have to write this sentence down 500 times before I can go home. I don't have time to argue. "I will not kick the cheerleaders."

RICH. What are you in for?

ANNE. Kicking the cheerleaders. Believe me, with their pouffy hair and pom-poms, they deserved my boot up their butts. "I will not kick the cheerleaders."

RICH. Oh yeah? Well, I'm in for kicking the janitor. He scrubbed my graffiti off the bathroom stalls. Janitor beats cheerleader. It's my seat!

ANNE. It's mine!

RICH. Mine!

ANNE. Mine!

RICH. You wanna fight?

ANNE. (*Stands.*) Bring it on, buddy boy!

(**RICH** *quickly parks himself in her former seat.*)

RICH. Ha, ha! Told you it was mine!

ANNE. Nobody tricks me!

RICH. Looks like I just did.

ANNE. I'll get you for that!

(*She goes to slug him, when* **EIGHT** *steps into the scene.*)

EIGHT. Freeze! (**EVERYONE** *freezes.*) Page 138. Enough already! The sooner you realize that you're all in the same boat, the sooner you can learn to get along. Though it may feel like you're all alone, being a freshman is not a solitary experience. Everyone is going through the same thing at the same time with the same worries. It's just a matter of sticking it out. Together. (*She intercepts the punch as* **EVERYONE** *unfreezes.*) Whoa, whoa, whoa! Time out!

ANNE. Let me at him! Let me at him!

EIGHT. What's wrong?

ANNE. He's in my seat! I'll leave the cheerleaders alone, but his butt is mine!

RICH. Then why don't you come and get me?

ANNE. You wouldn't stand a chance!

EIGHT. Come on, you. Cool off!

(*She plops* **ANNE** *down in a chair.* **ANNE** *pants furiously, but calms down.* **RICH** *sticks out his tongue at her and she growls.*)

RICH. Thanks. She's crazy.

EIGHT. That's right. (*She struts over to* **RICH**.) But so am I. Get out of my seat.

RICH. Huh?

EIGHT. You heard me. Out!

RICH. This isn't your seat.

EIGHT. I've been sitting in that seat for the past four years. Until I graduate, that seat is mine!

RICH. No it's not!

EIGHT. Yes it is!

ANNE. (*Stands up.*) No it's not!

EIGHT. You stay out of this!

ANNE. I won't stay out of it. What's the big idea here? Come on, Rich. You can't let her talk to you that way.

RICH. Why do you care?

ANNE. Just because she's a senior doesn't give her the right to push us freshmen around.

EIGHT. Who says?

ANNE. I says. We gotta stick together.

RICH. You're right. (*To* **EIGHT.**) This is my seat and there's nothing you can do about it!

EIGHT. Wanna bet?

RICH. (*Stands up.*) Bring it on!

EIGHT. You can't hurt me!

(**ANNE** *grabs* **EIGHT** *and swivels her around.*)

ANNE. But I can! Come on, Rich. Just because she's older, doesn't make her any better. Let's blow this joint.

RICH. What about your 500 lines?

ANNE. I'll worry about that later. There's a pep rally tomorrow, and we've got some serious planning to do. (*She puts her arm around him.*) Come on, pal.

(**RICH** *sticks his tongue out at* **EIGHT** *as they exit arm in arm.* **EIGHT** *smiles at the audience.*)

EIGHT. Works every time.

(*LIGHTS out. LIGHTS up DR, on* **ONE.**)

ONE. There you have it, freshmen. Advice you won't find in any book on any shelf in any Barnes and Noble.

(*LIGHTS up CS, on* TWO *through* EIGHT *standing in a line.* ONE *joins them.*)

ONE. (*Continued.*) Take what you've heard with a grain of salt.

TWO. But take it from us –

THREE. This stuff works.

FOUR. So the next time you're upset by a teacher –

FIVE. A bully –

SIX. Or even a friend –

SEVEN. And graduation seems a million miles away –

EIGHT. Remember what you've seen here tonight.

ONE. These are tricks of the trade –

TWO. Passed down from generation to generation –

THREE. From senior to freshmen.

FOUR. We went through it –

FIVE. So that you don't have to!

SIX. Just remember to live each day to the fullest, and you will never –

SEVEN. Ever –

EIGHT. Come anywhere close to being –

EVERYONE. A dummy!

(*LIGHTS out.*)

END OF PLAY

PROPS

"For Dummies" books
Textbooks
Notebooks
Lipstick
Tissues
Straw
Three basketballs
Two cafeteria trays
Nasty looking "mac and cheese"
Serving spoon
Dollar bills
Drama masks
Gum
Yard stick
Crumpled notes

OTHER TITLES AVAILABLE FROM BAKER'S PLAYS

JUST A HIGH SCHOOL PLAY

E. Eugene Perry

Drama / 6m, 12f / bare stage with props

There are presently 51,173,992 high school students in the United States, more or less, and here are eighteen representative characters. Anyone who's ever been to high school will recognize them all — the Jock, the Shy Kid, the Gossip, the Cheerleader, the Joker, the Brain, the New Kid, the Hunk, the Actress, the Trouble, the Observer, the Poet, the Reputation.

Just a High School Play deals with the thoughts and reflections of eighteen realistic and profoundly individualistic rural high school students as they approach the end of their senior year. Set in a small town high school, this series of scenes and monologues provides an age-appropriate acting challenge for students.

With simple staging and a flexible cast, this play lends itself to high school productions with limited space, time or budgets.

Contains mature language.

Printed in the USA
CPSIA information can be obtained
at www.ICGtesting.com
LVHW022057291123
765059LV00013B/943